ARE you SITTING Comfortably?

FOR MAX,
who I just
KNOW is going to
LOVE
books

Bloomsbury Publishing, London, Oxford, New York, New Delhi and Sydney
First published in Great Britain in 2016 by Bloomsbury Publishing Plc
50 Bedford Square, London WC1B 3DP

This paperback edition first published in 2017

www.bloomsbury.com

A CIP catalogue record of this book is available from the British Library

ISBN 978 1 4088 6482 1 (HB) ISBN 978 1 4088 6483 8 (PB) ISBN 978 1 4088 6481 4 (eBook)

All papers used by Bloomsbury Publishing are natural, recyclable products made from wood grown in well managed forests. The manufacturing processes conform to the environmental regulations of the country of origin.

Printed in China by C & C Offset Printing Co Ltd, Shenzhen, Guangdong

1 0 9 8 7 6 5 4 3 2 1

ARE you SITTING Comfortably?

Leigh Hodgkinson

BLOOMSBURY
LONDON OXFORD NEW YORK NEW DELHI SYDNEY

The thing is . . .

when I want to read,

what I REALLY

REALLY need

is a place to sit . . .

just for a bit.

ARE you
SITTING
Comfortably?

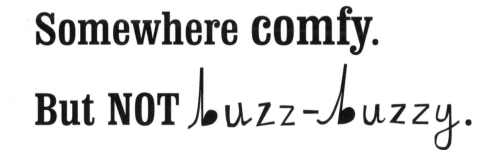

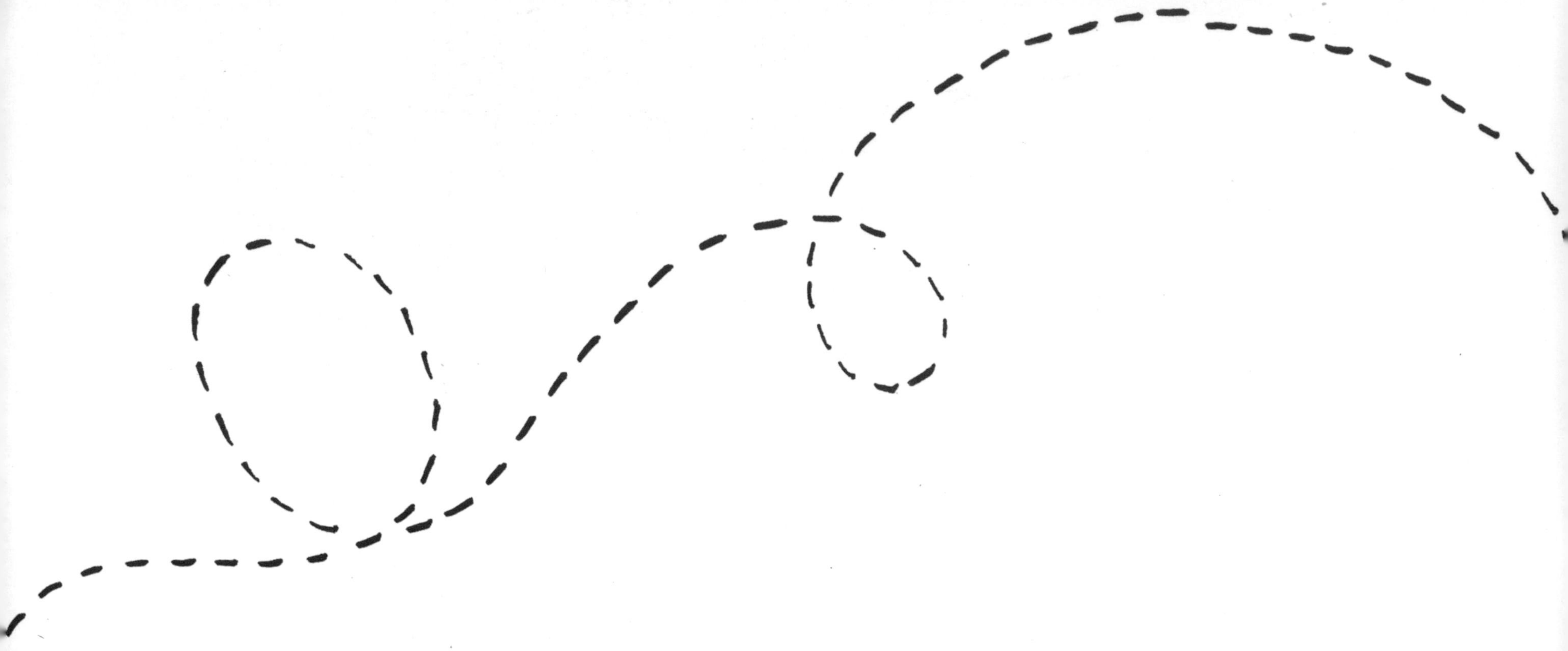

Somewhere comfy.

But NOT buzz-buzzy.

ARE you SITTING Comfortably?

And NOT all

growly, itchy,

FUZZY.

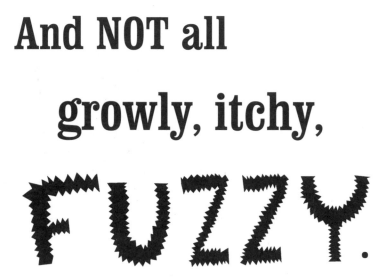

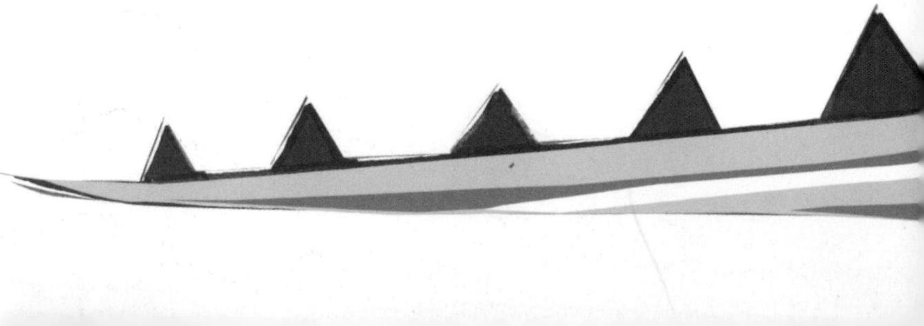

ARE you
SITTING
Comfortably?

Some place brighter.

WITHOUT these

HOOTS.

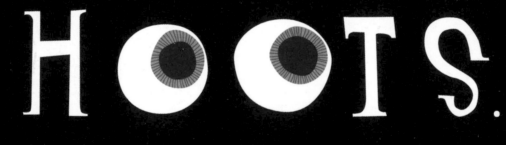

HOOT
HOOT

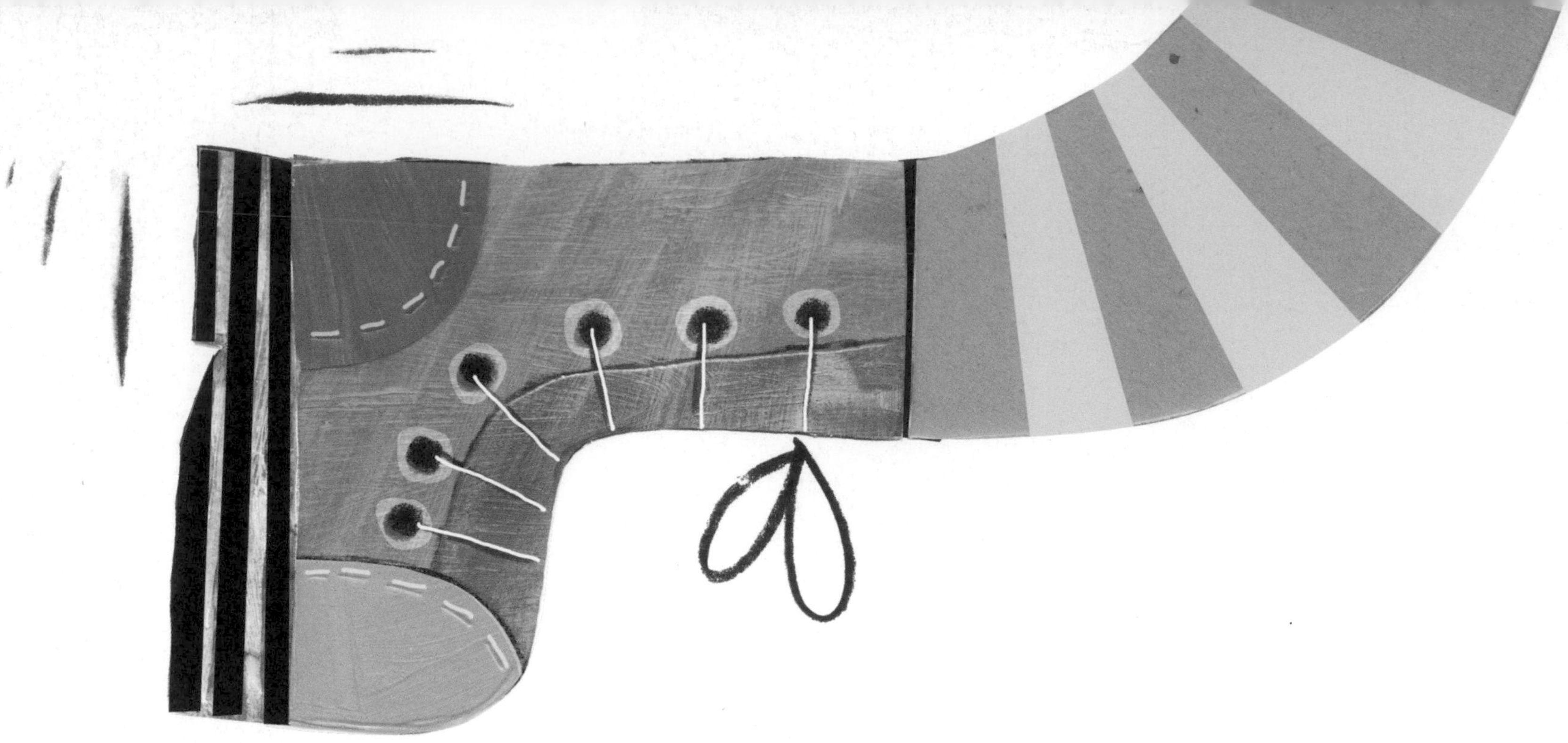

And 'NO!' to

GIANT

STOMPING boots.

A place NOT niffy,

stinky

grimy.

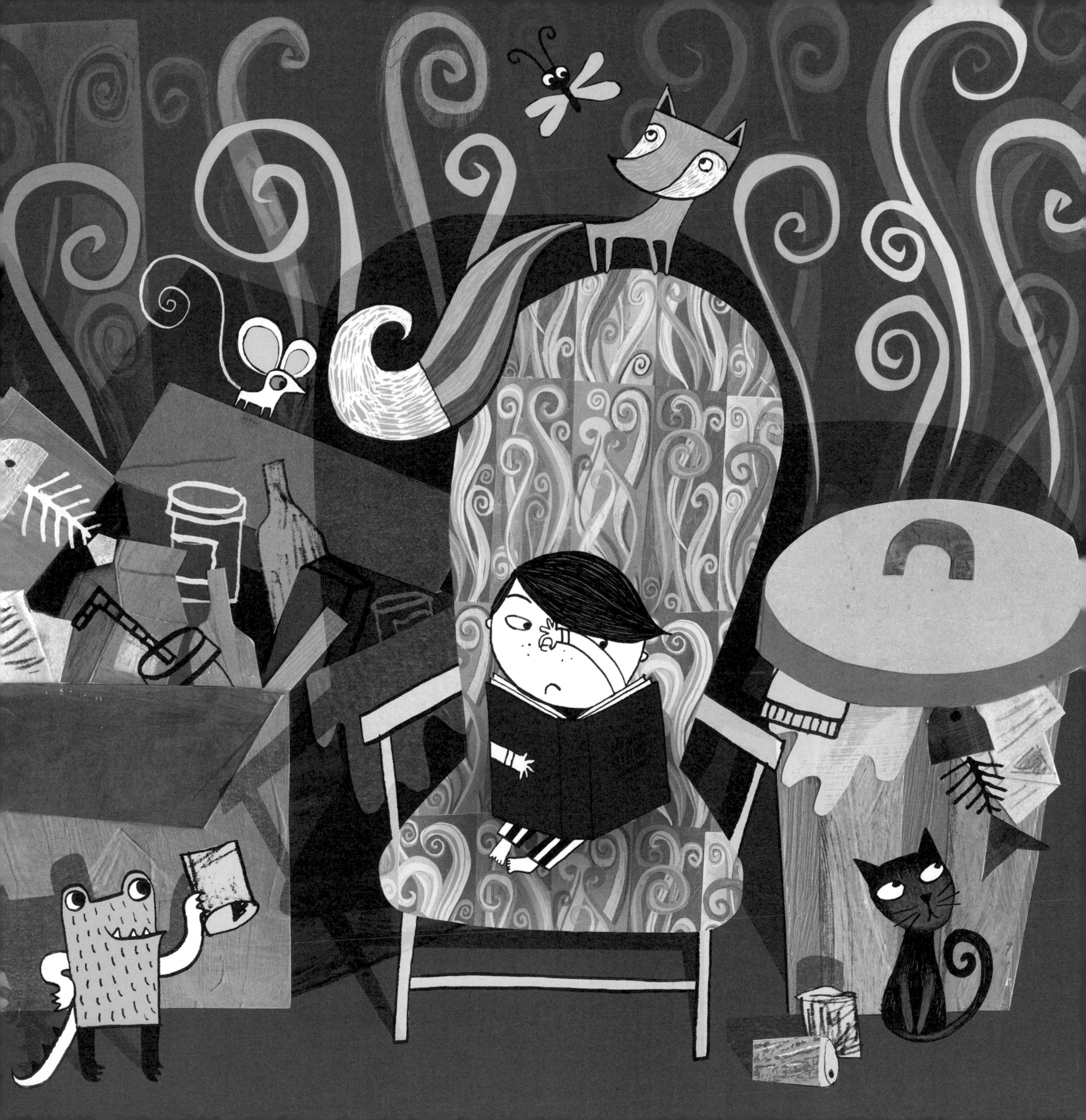

Somewhere nice. NOT *slippy*, slimy.

(And I don't like **soggy** – sorry, Froggy!)

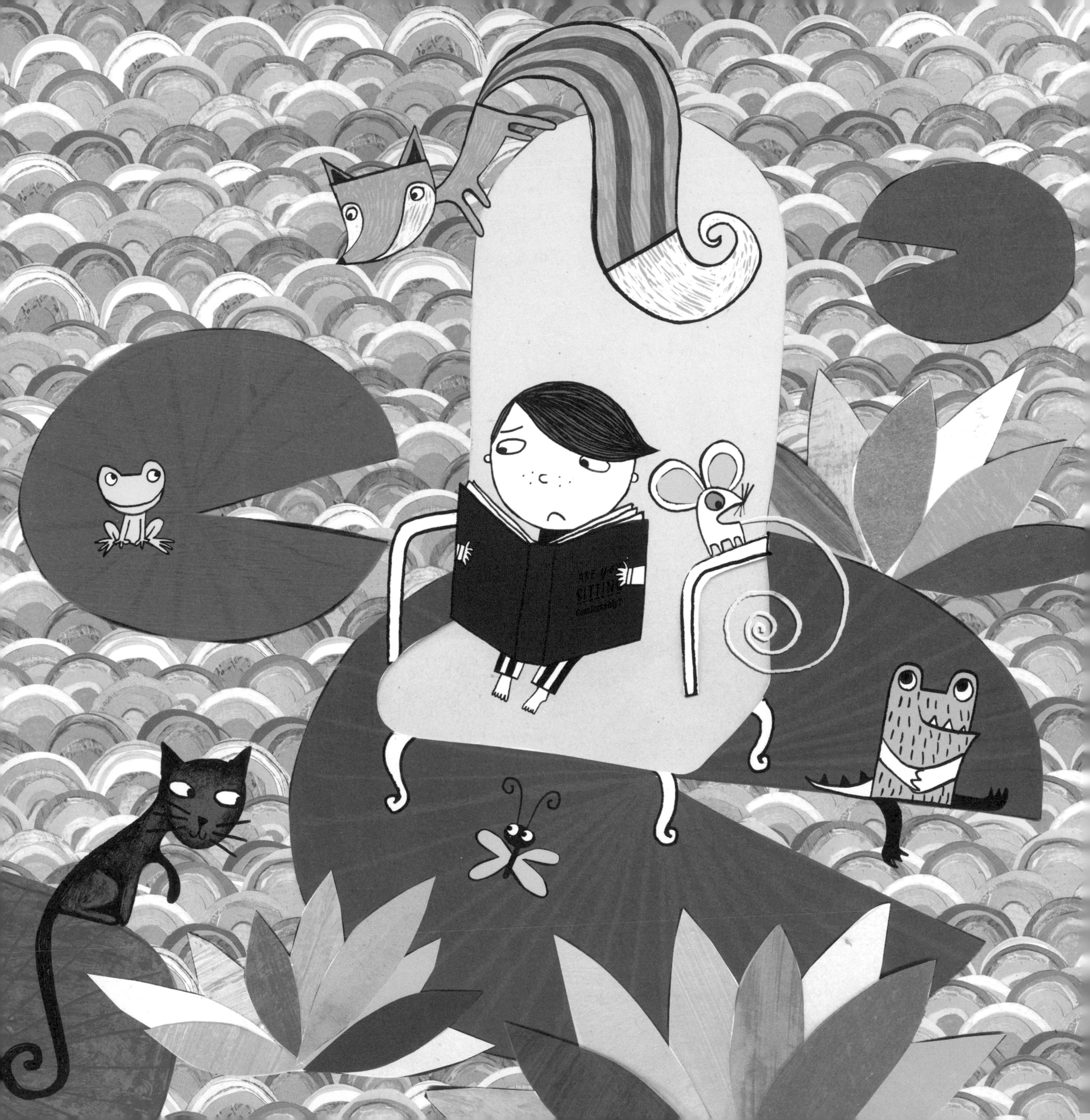
ARE
SITTING

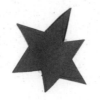

But it can't be far –

SORRY star!

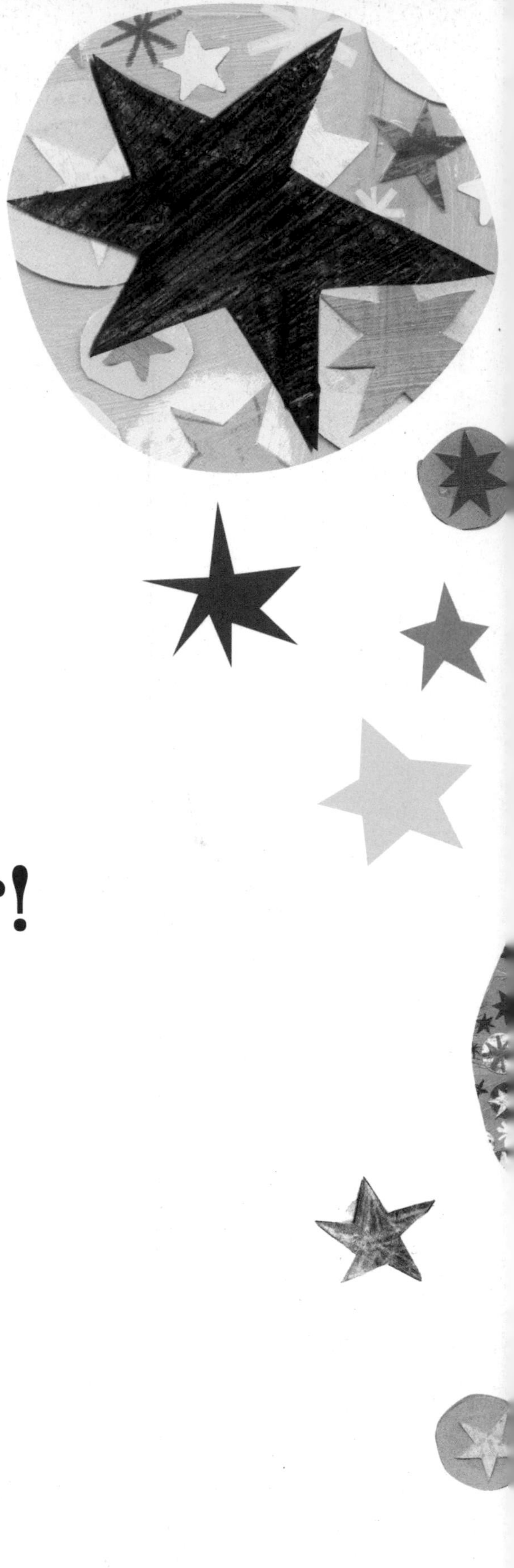

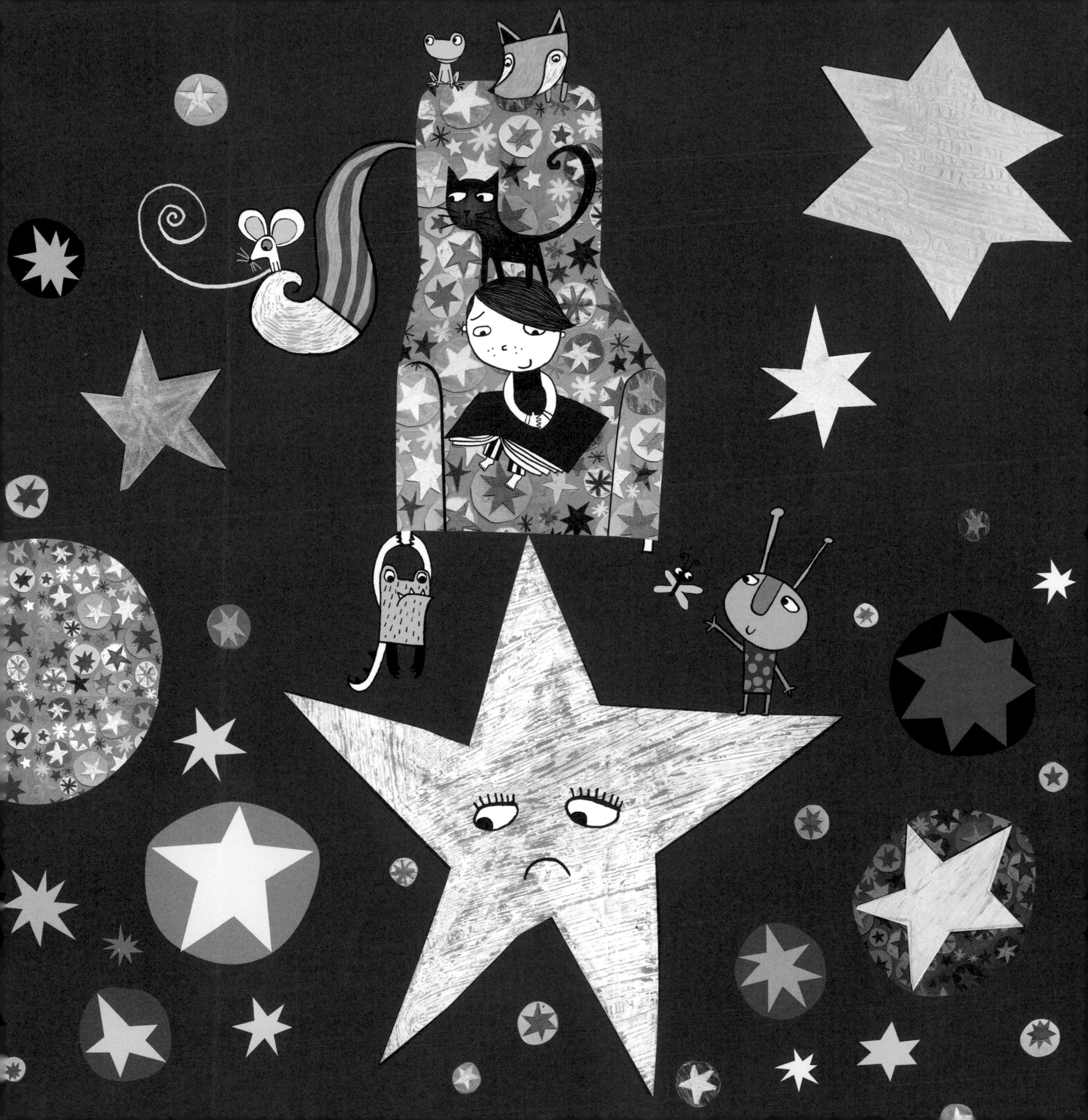

It's GOT

to be NOT hot, you see.

ARE you SITTING Comfortably?

And NOT too

cold...

. . . or up a TREE.

(This is WAY too high for me!)

ARE
comfortably?

Is this so very much to *ask*?

It seems to be a **MIGHTY** task.

But wait, hang on –

YES

THAT'S IT!

It doesn't matter

where you sit . . .

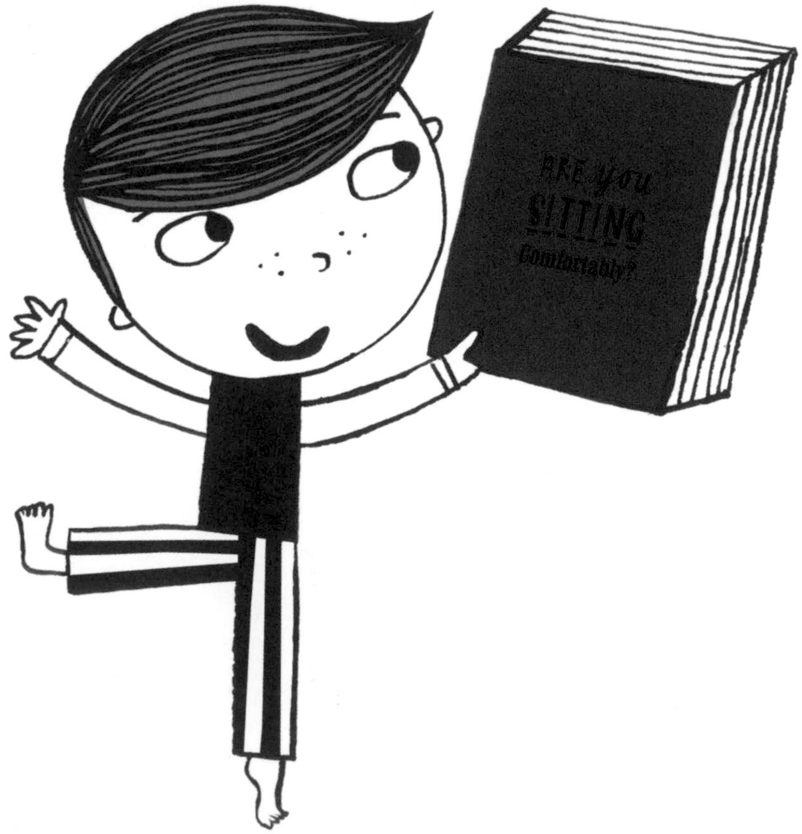

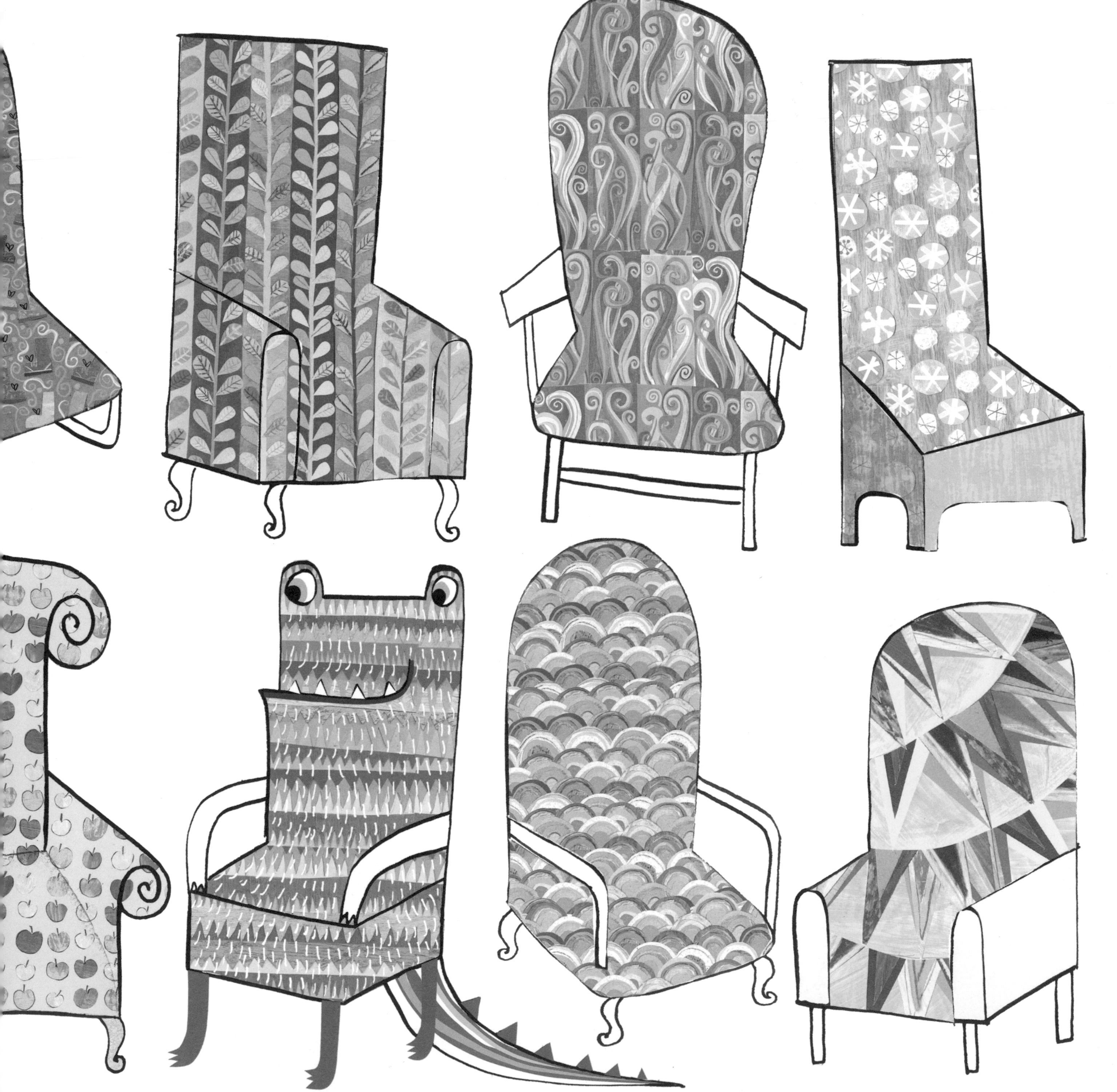

. . . a book is best *anywhere* . . .

a book is best when you

SHARE.

And the boy, the cat, the monster, the fox, the butterfly, the mouse, the frog, the martian, the lion, the polar bear and the bird…
All read happily EVER AFTER.